DON'T TOUCH
THAT!

Veronika Martenova Charles

Illustrated by David Parkins

Tundra Books

Tundra Books, a division of Random House of Canada Limited, a Penguin Random
House Company

Published simultaneously in the United States of America by Tundra Books of Northern
New York, a division of Random House of Canada Limited, a Penguin Random House
Company

Library of Congress Control Number: 2008920883

Library and Archives Canada Cataloguing in Publication

Charles, Veronika Martenova
    Don't touch that! / Veronika Martenova Charles ; illustrated by David Parkins.

(Easy-to-read spooky tales)
ISBN 978-0-88776-858-3

1. Horror tales, Canadian (English). 2. Children's stories, Canadian (English).
I. Parkins, David II. Title. III. Series: Charles, Veronika Martenova. Easy-to-read
spooky tales.

PS8555.H42242D675 2008   jC813'.54   C2007–907592–4

**ONTARIO ARTS COUNCIL
CONSEIL DES ARTS DE L'ONTARIO**

We acknowledge the financial support of the Government of Canada through the
Canada Book Fund and that of the Government of Ontario through the Ontario Media
Development Corporation's Ontario Book Initiative. We further acknowledge the
support of the Canada Council for the Arts and the Ontario Arts Council for our
publishing program.

Printed and bound in China

4 5 6 7 8   19 18 17 16

CONTENTS

THE CONSTRUCTION
PART I

"They are digging a road

near my house,"

I told Leon and Marcos.

"Let's go to my place

and we can watch."

I asked my mom if we could go.

"Yes, but don't touch anything!"

she said.

4

We sat on the sidewalk

and watched the men work.

They dug a ditch and laid a pipe

inside it. They put boards

around the hole,

and then they left for the day.

"Let's have a better look,"

said Leon. We went closer.

"What's that thing down there?"

Marcos pointed to an object.

It was sticking up

from the bottom of the ditch.

It was made of rusty metal.

"It's treasure!" said Marcos.

"Or maybe a bomb," said Leon.

"I bet someone put it there

so we would see it," I said.

"It's part of an evil plan!

I've heard a story like that.

It's about toys."

"Tell us that story,"

Leon and Marcos said.

THE TOYS

(My Story)

In a village, far, far up north,

lived two girls

called Suluk and Nukka.

One day, they went out to play

behind their igloos.

"Look at this!" said Suluk.

There, sticking out of the snow,

was a toy bird

carved out of bone.

"Don't touch that!" said Nukka.

"Who knows why it is there."

But Suluk took it, played with it,

and soon Nukka did too.

"Look! There is another toy!"

called Suluk again.

They dropped the toy bird

and went to see the next toy.

Then, they saw another,

and still another, farther along.

Suluk and Nukka followed

the toy trail farther and farther

from the village

to a house made of stones.

Suluk and Nukka walked in.

Even more toys were inside.

An old woman suddenly appeared.

She pushed Suluk and Nukka

farther inside, to another room.

Then, she took a large stone

and blocked the door.

Inside, there were more children

tied together with a rope.

"The woman is a witch!"

the children whispered.

"We can't run away.

The witch always catches us."

Suluk and Nukka made up a plan.

"I'll cut a hole in the wall

with a sharp toy,

while you make a noise,"

whispered Nukka

to the other children.

The children started to shout.

The witch checked on them,

but then she left to make a fire.

Nukka began to scrape the sand

around a stone in the wall.

15

When the stone came loose,

she pulled it out,

then she slid it back in place.

In the meantime,

Nukka untied the rope

around the children.

That night, Suluk told the witch,

"I would like to serve you

in any way I can.

Shall I cut your toenails?"

The witch took Suluk with her

into the other room.

Then she held out her foot.

Suluk cut the witch's toenails

and, quick as a wink, she tied

the rope around the witch's foot.

"It's done!" she called.

When the children heard her,

they took the stone out of the wall

and climbed outside.

Suluk ran into the other room,

squeezed through the hole,

and gave the rope to the children.

They all pulled on the rope

and dragged the witch

across the floor of her house.

When they got her to the wall,

she put her feet against it.

The children pulled harder.

CRASH!

The wall came tumbling down.

The stones fell on the witch

and killed her.

Suluk, Nukka, and the children

were free to return safely home.

Leon looked in the ditch again.

"You know what?" he said.

"I bet that thing can open

and there is something inside.

We could climb down

to get it and see."

"I don't think so," said Marcos.

"There could be an evil spirit.

I know a story like that.

Should I tell you?"

"Sure!" Leon and I said.

THE GLASS BOTTLE

(Marcos' Story)

"Today is Grandma's birthday,"

Mother said to Tim and Lara.

"Please go to visit her,

and take this box of chocolates.

I made sandwiches for you

to eat along the way."

Tim put the box of chocolates

in his knapsack,

and he and Lara started out.

To get to their grandma's village,

they had to go through a forest.

The sun was shining,

and Tim and Lara

skipped along the path.

Suddenly, Tim stopped.

He saw something shiny lying

at the base of a big oak tree.

He went to look at it.

A glass bottle was sticking

out of the ground.

"I found a bottle!" Tim shouted.

"Don't touch that!" Laura said.

They walked a little bit farther.

"Let's have lunch." Laura said.

She sat down

and pulled out her sandwich.

"I'll be right back.

I want to look around first,"

said Tim.

While his sister rested,

Tim went back to the big oak tree

to look at the bottle again.

When he found it,

he pulled it out of the ground.

There was something inside,

and it jumped up and down.

Tim heard a tiny voice crying,

"Let me out! Let me out!"

Tim opened the bottle.

The thing came out,

and it began to grow fast.

It became an ugly giant,

half as big as the oak tree.

"Now," the giant roared,

"give me what you have!"

Tim gave him his sandwich.

"What else is in your knapsack?"

the giant asked.

"There is a box of chocolates

for my grandma," Tim answered.

"Give it to me!"

"I can't." Tim's voice shook.

"It's her birthday present."

"Give it to me,

or I will wring your neck!"

the giant commanded.

Now Tim was angry.

"You big bully,

what makes you think

you're so special?" he said.

"I don't think you came

from this little bottle at all.

You're a fake!" said Tim.

"Oh yeah?" roared the giant.

"Just watch this!"

And the giant began to shrink

until he was able to squeeze

back inside of the bottle.

The moment the giant was inside,

Tim shoved the cork

back into the bottle.

"Let me out! Let me out!"

a voice cried from the bottle.

"Not a chance!" said Tim.

Tim buried the bottle again

in the roots of the oak tree.

Then, he rushed back

to where Lara was waiting,

and they continued on their way

to their grandma's village.

★ ★ ★

"I would love to see a giant

squeezing into a bottle," I said.

"It could have been worse,"

said Leon.

"There could have been a monster

underneath the bottle.

I'll tell you a story like that.

It's called *The Dragon*."

THE DRAGON

(Leon's Story)

There was a mother

who had a daughter called Alma.

To make their living,

they picked cabbages

and sold them.

One day, as they worked

in the field,

Alma spied an enormous cabbage.

She showed it to her mother.

"Don't touch that!" said the mother.

"It doesn't look right.

Get away from it!"

But Alma stayed behind

and pulled up the huge cabbage.

There was a hole underneath it,

and in it was a trapdoor.

Alma climbed down,

opened the trapdoor,

and found an underground room.

A dragon was sitting in a chair.

"Mmmm! I smell human flesh!"

the dragon said.

"Please don't eat me!" said Alma.

"Well, I'll think about that,"

said the dragon.

"I'm going hunting now."

"You look after my place.

For your dinner, I'm leaving you

a human hand."

Alma was frightened.

How can I eat a human hand?

she thought. But she replied,

"Yes sir, Dragon. I will eat it."

After the dragon left,

Alma took the hand,

threw it in a bucket,

and poured water over it.

"Now it's gone," she sighed.

"The dragon will think I ate it."

Then, the dragon returned.

"Did you eat the hand?" he asked.

"Yes, it was tasty," Alma said.

"Let's see," said the dragon.

"Hand, where are you?"

"In the bucket!" came a voice.

The dragon grabbed Alma.

"You lied!" the dragon told her.

"Now you will be punished."

"Please," pleaded Alma,

"can I have one more chance?"

"All right," the dragon agreed.

"You eat this foot

while I go hunting again."

"Yes sir, Dragon," Alma replied.

After the dragon left,

Alma had an idea.

She put the foot in her stocking

and tied it around her stomach

under her clothes.

When the dragon returned,

he asked Alma,

"Did you eat the foot?"

And Alma answered,

"It's on my stomach."

"Let's see," said the dragon.

"Foot, where are you?" he yelled.

And the foot replied,

"I'm on Alma's stomach!"

"Hurrah!" shouted the dragon.

"Now I'm going to . . ."

THE CONSTRUCTION
PART 2

"Look!" said Marcos.

"Your mom is coming.

Maybe we should tell her

about the thing in the ditch."

We went to meet her halfway.

"You've been here awhile,"

said my mother.

"We were talking," we told her.

"Can we show you something?"

We led her to the ditch

and showed her the object.

My mom looked at it and said,

"I'm going to call someone.

Let's go away from here."

At home, my mom called 911.

A police car came.

The policemen went to the ditch

and we saw them using

their walkie-talkies.

Then, an armored truck arrived.

Two men jumped out,

dressed like spacemen.

The police came to our door.

"Everyone stay inside," they said.

"What is it?" my mom asked.

"It's a rusty old shell casing;

likely an old war souvenir.

There's no need to worry.

We'll take care of it," they said.

We watched through the window.

The "spacemen" came back,

carrying a heavy box.

They loaded it into the truck,

and then the truck drove off.

"All clear," the officers said.

"It was good not to touch that,

and to tell your mom, instead!

You guys are heroes."

It felt great, but I wondered:

What else might be in the ditch?

AFTERWORD

What do you think

the dragon was about to do

at the end of his story?

Was he going to eat Alma?

Let her go? Make her eat

something else?

Have fun finishing the story

any way you like.

WHERE THE STORIES COME FROM

The Toys is an Inuit tale, but here,

I have let the children

carry out their own rescue.

The Glass Bottle comes from

a German folktale.

The Dragon is based on

an Italian fairy tale.

The story about finding

a shell during construction

actually happened

in my very own backyard!